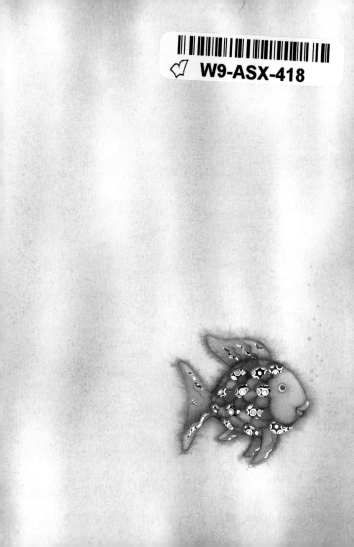

Don't miss the other books in this series:
RAINBOW FISH TO THE RESCUE!
RAINBOW FISH AND THE BIG, BLUE WHALE

First mini-book edition published in the United States, Great Britain,
Canada, Australia and New Zealand in 1999 by North-South Books,
an imprint of Nord-Süd Verlag AG, Gossau Zürich, Switzerland.

ISBN 0-7358-1222-5
1 3 5 7 9 10 8 6 4 2
Prinded in Italy

MARCUS PFISTER
THE RAINBOW FISH

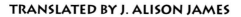

TRANSLATED BY J. ALISON JAMES

NORTH-SOUTH BOOKS / NEW YORK / LONDON

A long way out in the deep blue sea there lived a fish. Not just an ordinary fish, but the most beautiful fish in the entire ocean. His scales were every shade of blue and green and purple, with sparkling silver scales among them.

The other fish were amazed at his beauty. They called him Rainbow Fish. "Come on, Rainbow Fish," they would call. "Come and play with us!" But the Rainbow Fish would just glide past, proud and silent, letting his scales shimmer.

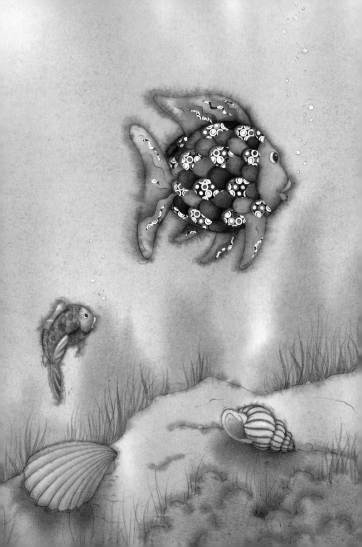

One day, a little blue fish followed after him. "Rainbow Fish," he called, "wait for me! Please give me one of your shiny scales. They are so wonderful, and you have so many."

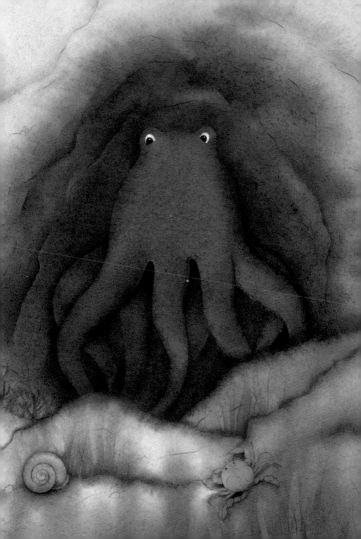

"I have been waiting for you," said the octopus with a deep voice. "The waves have told me your story. This is my advice. Give a glittering scale to each of the other fish. You will no longer be the most beautiful fish in the sea, but you will discover how to be happy."

"I can't..." the Rainbow Fish started to say, but the octopus had already disappeared into a dark cloud of ink.

Give away my scales? My beautiful shining scales? Never. How could I ever be happy without them?

Suddenly he felt the light touch of a fin. The little blue fish was back!

"Rainbow Fish, please, don't be angry. I just want one little scale."

The Rainbow Fish wavered. Only one very very small shimmery scale, he thought. Well, maybe I wouldn't miss just one.

Carefully the Rainbow Fish pulled out the smallest scale and gave it to the little fish.

"Thank you! Thank you very much!" The little blue fish bubbled playfully, as he tucked the shiny scale in among his blue ones.

A rather peculiar feeling came over the Rainbow Fish. For a long time he watched the little blue fish swim back and forth with his new scale glittering in the water.

The little blue fish whizzed through the ocean with his scale flashing, so it didn't take long before the Rainbow Fish was surrounded by the other fish. Everyone wanted a glittering scale. The Rainbow Fish shared his scales left and right. And the more he gave away, the more delighted he became. When the water around him filled with glimmering scales, he at last felt at home among the other fish.

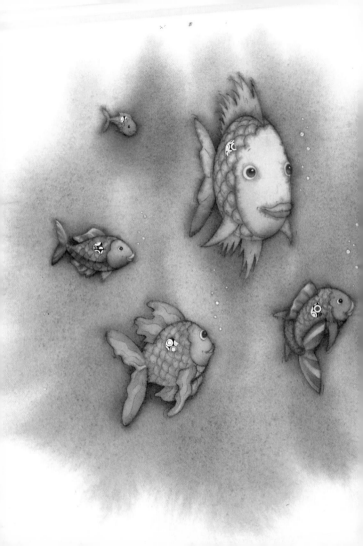

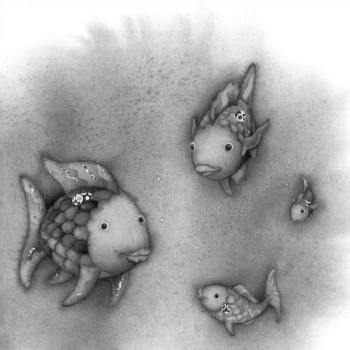

Finally the Rainbow Fish had only one shining scale left. His most prized possessions had been given away, yet he was very happy.

"Come on, Rainbow Fish," they called. "Come and play with us!"

"Here I come," said the Rainbow Fish, and happy as a splash, he swam off to join his friends.